D0416501

This book belongs to:

_____

_____

_____

First published 2000 by Walker Books Ltd
87 Vauxhall Walk, London SE11 5HJ

8 10 9 7

© 2000 Lucy Cousins

Maisy™. Maisy is a registered trademark of Walker Books Ltd, London.

Based on the Audio Visual Series "Maisy". A King Rollo Fims Production for
Universal Pictures Visual Programming. Original Script by Andrew Brenner.

This book has been typeset in Lucy Cousins typeface

Printed in China

British Library Cataloguing in Publication Data:
a catalogue record for this book is
available from the British Library

ISBN 978-0-7445-7278-0

www.walkerbooks.co.uk

Maisy's Bus

LUTON LIBRARIES BOROUGH COUNCIL	
938972218	
JP	PETERS
17-Jun-2008	LY

Lucy Cousins

WALKER BOOKS

AND SUBSIDIARIES

LONDON · BOSTON · SYDNEY · AUCKLAND

Maisy is driving her bus today.

Who will be at bus stop number 1?

It's Cyril.

Hello, Cyril.

Little Black cat
is waiting at bus
stop number 2.

Hello,
Little Black cat.

Brmm, brmm!

Who will be at bus stop number 3?

It's Tallulah,
waiting in the rain.

Hello, Tallulah.

Eddie is waiting at bus stop number 4.

Will there be room on the bus?

Hooray! There's room for everyone.

Brmm, brmm! Where is Maisy going now?

Bus stop number 5.

It's time to get off, everyone.

Oops! Wake up,
Little Black Cat.

This is the last stop.

Bye bye, everyone.
Bye bye, Maisy.

Brmm, brmm!

If you're crazy for Maisy, you'll love these books featuring Maisy and her friends.

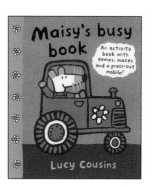

Other titles
Maisy's ABC • Maisy Goes to Bed • Maisy Goes to the Playground
Maisy Goes Swimming • Maisy Goes to Playschool
Maisy's House • Happy Birthday, Maisy • Maisy at the Farm